True Feathers

by

Shirley Tolbert-Madden

True Feathers

Illustrator: Brenda Stroud

Book Layout: SOS Graphics and Printing

Publisher: G Publishing LLC
            Detroit, Michigan

ISBN 13: 978-0-9820002-6-7
    10: 0-9820002-6-X

Library of Congress Control Number: 2008911356

Published and Printed in the United States of America

Bosco woke up late one morning. His family was gone. He did not listen to his mother's warning about sleeping so late. Now, lonely and scared, he sat hidden on a high branch of a tall pine tree, over a lake where children were splish-splashing in the water.

Bosco was scared. He flew up and down, fast and slow hoping to find his family. Then he heard a pleasant sound but it wasn't his mother's. It said, "Coo, coo."

Landing in a tree, he thought, I will be a bird just like you, until I know I can be true. He scrunched his body into a ball and thought real hard and then, KA-POOF , he looked and sounded just like the mourning dove.

Bosco puffed out his chest of soft gray feathers and cooed, "I am a mourning dove just like you."

The doves slowly circled around Bosco, looking at him strangely. Then, one dove cooed loudly, "You're not like us." He saw Bosco's big beak.

Another dove cooed, "Go away from us."
Bosco flew away quickly. He wanted to be in their family so the mother could bring him some food because that's what his mother did. Now he was lonely and hungry.

Suddenly two birds came walking up the bark of the tree. "Kwee, kwee," they called. They were woodpeckers called flickers.

Once again Bosco scrunched his body into a tight ball and thought, I will be a bird just like you, until I know I can be true. Then KA-POOF, he cleared his throat and called out, "Kwee, kwee."

His feathers changed to a yellowish color with bands of black across his back and black spots on his chest. He looked just like the flickers sitting next to him, except for his large beak.

"I'm just like you," screeched a happy Bosco.

"Really?" questioned one of the flickers in his kwee-kwee voice. Leaning his head, he glanced at Bosco's long and strange beak. "Well, we're going to eat now, so come with us."

They all flapped down to the ground. The flickers started eating
ants.

Bosco picked up an ant with his large beak but it crawled out and walked up his beak to his eyes. Shaking his head back and forth to make the ant fall off, he thought it was disgusting to eat ants anyway. Giving a mighty thrust of his wings, off he went again, hungry and still lonely.

Bosco weeped, Where is my family? He flew from tree to tree trying to find them.

On his search, he met a red cardinal. Bosco scrunched his body into a ball and thought, I will be a bird just like you, until I know I can be true. KA-POOF ! Now Bosco looked just like the cardinals, even with a tuft of red feathers on the top of his head. "Chew, chew, chew, Tiw, tiw, tiw." The cardinal flew up to him and looked at him strangely. Bosco was bigger but he still looked like him, except for that long beak.

The cardinal flew to a low branch and chirped loudly at Bosco in his chew-chew, tiw, tiw voice. "Fly away bird. Go back to your home. You are not a cardinal, so leave us alone."

This made Bosco sad, so he flapped slowly away from the cardinals. Sitting on a branch in a large oak tree he thought for sure that looking and sounding like the other birds would be enough to welcome him into their family. But he was wrong.

He had gone all morning with no food. Searching for his family was hard work. Flying over neighborhoods, he saw children outside playing, parents taking care of their lawns and birds pecking at the ground. Oops! Bosco stopped flying in mid-air. There are some birds.

He flew to a branch and scrunched his body into a ball. I will be a bird just like you, until I know I can be true. KA-POOF ! The feathers on his back turned a darker brown while his chest was a bright red.

The robins gave a warm hello to Bosco. They all clucked, "Piik, piik, piik, piik." Bosco felt happy to be accepted into the robin family. Pecking at the ground, he finally pulled up a wiggling worm. His large beak could not hold it and the worm wiggled right out.

Another robin came over and gobbled down the worm. "Pup, pup, pup," meant, "Thanks for helping me get my food."

Bosco didn't want to eat a wiggling worm anyway. The robin chirped to Bosco, "You are a nice bird, find the food that will make you happy."

"Okay," tweeted Bosco flapping good-bye to Mr. Robin. As he soared in the air, he gave a long and loud wail, 'Father, Mother, where are you?'

As Bosco continued flying, he spotted a pair of blue jays. He sat on a branch and scrunched his body into a ball. I will be a bird just like you, until I know I can be true. His feathers turned the same shade as the deep blue ocean. He even had a tuft of blue feathers on the crown of his head. The male blue jay looked at him and screamed out angrily, "Ja-a-a-a-a-y," which meant, "Go away."

They were eating little insects and seeds. Bosco walked behind them,
pecking but getting nothing in his large beak.
Imitating the sound of the blue jay, he said, "Jaaa-aaa-aaa-aay,"
which meant "I am just like you."

The blue jay called back in a shrill voice, "Jaaaaa-aaa-aaaaa-aaa-ay," and wanted Bosco to know, "You are not like me." Then the blue jay flew over and pecked Bosco on the top of his head.

"Ow-w-w," screamed Bosco not sounding at all like a blue jay. He quickly flew away from Mr. Jay and rested on a branch in a nearby tree. He used one of his long wings to rub his sore head.

The next morning, Bosco decided not to sleep late. He was up early in search for food and his family. He flew over a large body of water. Looking down, he saw small fish swimming around. His stomach churned. He felt happy.

All of a sudden, he knew that was the food for him. As he started
a dive down towards the water, he saw the reflection of a beautiful
bird. It was mostly blue with some red and white on it. The wings
on the bird were quite large. "What a magnificent looking bird," he
thought. Then he realized, "That bird is me."

Bosco, looking like a jet, aimed his beak right into the water. Down he went without making a splash. It was perfect. He knew just what to do.

When he came up, he had a fish in his beak. He ate. Then he gave a happy chirp. This food was so good, down he went again. He came up with another fish. Giving a couple of flaps with his wings, he flew higher and higher and chirped louder and louder. He loved the sound of his own voice. He stopped to listen carefully. He heard a familiar song far away.

He began to fly towards the sound. It got louder and louder. It was his mother! "Keee, keee," she said, "Welcome home, Bosco."

He gave a gentle peck on his mother's head and said, "Keee, keee, keee, keee." "Mother, I was scared and didn't think I would ever see you again."

Before long, other birds that looked and sounded just like him were fluttering around him. They chirped together and played together. They called, "Ke-ke-ke-ke-ke," which meant, "We are kingfishers." Bosco rattled back, "Ke-ke-ke-ke," saying, "I am a kingfisher."

The other birds flew around Bosco. "Ke-ke-ke-ke-ke" or 'We're happy you're home."

Bosco soared high and he plunged low. He gave a loud squawk for all the other birds around to hear. I will not change to be like you, I know myself and I will be true. Now, Bosco was a happy bird in his true feathers.

Shirley Tolbert-Madden received her Ph.D. in Educational Psychology from the Union University in Cincinnati, Ohio. Her other degrees in Guidance and Counseling and Teaching were from Wayne State University in Detroit. As a licensed counselor, she has worked in private practice and in the Detroit Public Schools. She has published many in-house newsletters and authored several articles for parents pertaining to guidance. Dr. Madden lives in Detroit, Michigan with her husband, Gary, and son, Philip. True Feathers is her first book for children.

An array of subjects and choices of mediums are unveiled in Brenda Denby Stroud's body of work. Her primary focus has been "images from within" which combine pen and ink techniques, collage, and construction. Her choice of colors range from watercolor and acrylics through pastels. The images dictate the media with careful rendering of fine textures that capture the frequent mood swings and spontaneity in her work bringing excitement and interest to the viewer. Brenda's work "Challenge", "The Royal Couple", "Family Icon", and "Press On" were featured by GMC at National Urban League Conferences, and the Congressional Black Caucus. "Heritage", an acrylic collage, echoes the achievement and contribution of the African American to the automobile industry which encompasses building, designing and manufacturing. In the same spirit, "Diversity" highlights the contribution made by a diverse and unique ensemble of people who have been a pivotal force in the evolution of the automobile.

Printed in the United States
143216LV00001B